...in the deepest and most remote depths of thought, human depravity nestles...

...Ellipsis...

Tito Lugo MD©

1

Police officer Darío Rivera was known for his impressive precision with his 9mm Glock pistol. Wherever he set his sights, the bullet would hit. However, he had never used his weapon to take the life of another human being. His targets were only for practice, and occasionally, a chicken or other animal that ventured onto his private farm, located in the remote central regions of the island. The sound of his shots couldn't be heard for ten miles around, thanks to an illegal silencer he had confiscated from a criminal in the past and had decided to keep hidden for himself. Little could he imagine that he would soon use it to confront a cruel smuggler who killed newborns.

Raised in the heart of the island, this countryman found himself immersed in a dense forest, standing out as a unique detail amidst extraordinary circumstances, as if he were breathing fresh air in the center of bustling New York City. Unlike his grandmother, a native of the Big Apple, this countryman had never set foot in the city. He joined the police ranks as a detective due to his innate cunning and bravery. He took pleasure in unraveling the most complex mysteries that came his way.

Darío's superior, Chief Segismundo Aponte, was a potbellied, drunken fifty-eight-year-old man, with almost forty years of service in the police force. Despite his title of lieutenant colonel, his excessive alcohol consumption had caused brain damage, which kept him oblivious to much of what happened at the station. Sitting at his desk, overwhelmed by the mountain of paperwork he had to review and sign, he received news of the disappearance of a ten-day-old newborn from his parents' home in the Caguana neighborhood of Utuado. Caguana was in what seemed to be the end of the world, a place so remote it seemed to be in another galaxy. It could only be accessed through a narrow local road that barely fit a car. On this road, widenings formed due to the waiting of one vehicle to give way to another.

On that rainy February morning, the town's mayor called to inform him that during the early hours, Pancho and Samara's newborn had been kidnapped. The baby, a beautiful male child born by vaginal delivery ten days earlier and weighing six pounds, had already been nicknamed "Panchito," in honor of his father. The couple was bewildered by what happened, as they couldn't understand how the incident had occurred.

As reported, Pancho and Samara were sleeping together in the same bed when, between three and four in the morning, they heard a noise in their modest home. When they got up to investigate, they discovered that Panchito's crib was empty. At first, they thought it was a tasteless joke by friends, but when the child did not appear after three hours, and they did not hear his usual morning crying, they decided to contact the mayor. To do this, they had to drive three miles to the nearest gas station to use the public telephone. At six in the morning, the grocery store clerk at the station lent them her cell phone to call the town hall and alert the mayor about the kidnapping.

The mayor, in turn, called the lieutenant colonel in charge of the town's station, the disheveled drunkard Segismundo Aponte, to inform him of the baby's theft. In his usual indolence, Segismundo called officer Rivera, who immediately showed up at the station.

Upon arrival, his superior berated him, asking where he had been and why he was not aware of the kidnapping. Darío explained that he was practicing with his weapon, eliminating some stray dogs that were dirtying the area with their feces. This only angered the lieutenant colonel more, who immediately sent him to hell to investigate the kidnapping of the couple in the Caguana neighborhood.

"What the hell were you doing, Rivera?" Aponte growled, with his eyes narrowed in fury. "I was practicing shooting, chief. I wasn't expecting..." Darío started. "Wait a minute!" Aponte interrupted. "I don't care what you were expecting. This is serious, Rivera. There's a missing baby, and I need you to take action."

Forty-five minutes later, Darío arrived at Pancho and Samara's home, who were distraught over the inexplicable disappearance of their son. After inspecting the house and finding no evidence, Darío interviewed the parents about the people who had been near them in the last forty-eight hours. At first, they hesitated, but then they remembered a new vegetable seller in the neighborhood who had sold them products and had particularly recommended fresh coconut water. Both had drunk from it: Pancho with ice and whisky; Samara just with ice. After drinking, both felt a deep sleep and slept all night, side by side after having breastfed Panchito. When they woke up, they discovered that the child was not in his crib.

"A vegetable seller, you say?" asked Darío, frowning

"Yes, he was a young, friendly guy, with a disheveled beard. He sold us some produce and recommended the coconut water. But I don't think it has anything to do with it..." Samara replied, with a hint of doubt in her voice.

"Everything is relevant in an investigation," said Darío firmly. "Thank you for the information. I'll need it to move forward with this."

Darío, always astute, took the couple to the police forensic lab, where they had blood samples taken to check for possible intoxications.

"I want you to know that we are doing everything we can to find your son," Darío assured them, looking at them compassionately, "We need to be meticulous in our investigation."

Pancho and Samara nodded with somber gestures, clinging to the hope that their son would return safe and sound.

Meanwhile, Darío requested photographs of the baby and any characteristics that might help identify him.

"Do you remember any special details?" Darío asked, reviewing his notes.

"Panchito had a red mole on his left forearm," Samara replied, her voice choked with anguish, "The doctor said it was nothing serious, but it was our little unique detail."

"I understand," Darío nodded, taking note, "That could be useful."

With the information in hand, Darío distributed the photos to small stores and pharmacies that sold diapers and baby formula milk, in case someone bought them in the hours following the kidnapping.

"I hope this helps us find some clue," Darío murmured to himself, feeling the pressure of time on his shoulders.

A pharmacy in a nearby town reported that they had seen a young couple buying diapers and baby formula powder the day after the kidnapping. The security cameras at the pharmacy captured images of the couple.

"Can I see the recordings?" Darío asked, determination in his voice.

Although they checked the criminal database, they found no evidence identifying them as criminals. Four more pharmacies reported diaper purchases two days after the kidnapping, without providing clues about the missing baby or connections to previous crimes.

Days passed and Panchito's parents became increasingly desperate, not receiving any news or ransom demands. A month went by without any developments, leaving the couple shattered after nine months of hope and joy.

Darío was upset with himself for not finding any clues. However, a month after the kidnapping, a plastic bag with pediatric human remains was found. It was a fourteen-day-old baby that had died approximately two weeks earlier.

"This is terrible," Darío murmured, horrified by the macabre discovery.

The coroner took charge of the baby's body, and the director of the forensic institute was petrified when examining the remains.

"I can't believe what I see," she whispered, her eyes filled with tears.

The baby's body had a precise longitudinal surgical incision from the chin to the neck, in the center of the body, continuing to the pubic bone. The thyroid, carotid, superior vena cava, heart, and lungs had been precisely removed. The abdomen was devoid of organs, displaying precise and meticulous cuts. The face was emaciated and decomposed due to the action of time and other elements, making it almost impossible to identify the newborn. The eye sockets were missing.

The peculiar thing about the situation was that the empty body cavities had been hastily sealed with horse sewing thread, although the stitches were notably precise, forming a double "u". In the left corner of the inside of the abdominal cavity, what appeared to be a letter, possibly the letter "J," separated by three dots, was carved, although certainty about this was not guaranteed.

Talking to a pathologist colleague, the director of the forensic institute mentioned the case, and her colleague recalled similar cases of organ donation due to brain death. The baby had a round hemangioma on his left forearm, information that Darío shared with Panchito's parents. Seeing the mark, the parents identified the deceased baby as their son and plunged into inconsolable weeping. Peace fled from their future lives.

Darío carefully examined the doping tests performed on Pancho and Samara, finding traces of sodium thiopental, a barbiturate commonly known as sodium thiopental, with an ultra-short duration.

"This could explain the drowsiness they experienced," Darío murmured, slowly connecting the dots.

In the past, this substance had been used as a truth serum in interrogations and police interviews. Sodium thiopental produces sedative and depressant effects on the central nervous system, which would explain the drowsiness experienced by Panchito's parents on the night of the kidnapping. At least, there was a clue pointing to the macabre involvement of the vegetable seller.

With their hearts shattered, Panchito's parents submitted to the designs of the station's artist to create a sketch of the only character related to this atrocious event.

"I hope this brings us closer to finding who did this to our son," Pancho whispered, his voice broken by grief.

Darío nodded solemnly, feeling the weight of responsibility on his shoulders.

As the mayor was about to validate his position in the elections, he chose not to give too much coverage to this kidnapping and death, lest he lose votes from his fellow party members.

These locals from isolated communities became a constant annoyance for the mayor. They lived so far away, and the municipality had to bear the cost of installing pipes to provide them with light and potable water. On countless occasions, the mayor questioned why he should assume these expenses for people who didn't even participate in the elections. He would prefer that they gradually disappeared without causing a fuss, thus closing these outstanding accounts. As for the disappearance of his own son, the mayor cared little, as he believed that everyone is responsible for their actions. If there was no solution, there was no solution, the official thought with his limited capacity for reflection.

The vegetable seller never returned to the town. Over time, the case was filed in the police records without resolution, until something similar happened three months later in the mountainous area of the island.

2

Julio and Rosalinda met during their high school years, sharing a unique connection due to their reserved nature and minimal interaction with their peers. Despite their limited communication, they formed a couple that understood each other with just a sign, creating a perfect autistic dynamic.

Julio's childhood was marked by abuse inflicted by his parents, who imposed various punishments on him throughout his development. Both parents were alcoholics and never showed any interest in having children; Julio was considered a nuisance to them. Despite these adversities, he managed to persevere in his studies and enrolled in medical school, where he graduated as a doctor. He then began a residency in general surgery with the goal of specializing in organ transplantation. However, his career was abruptly cut short when he was expelled in the fourth year of residency due to unconventional practices and procedures that did not follow established surgical protocol.

Julio gained notoriety as a resident for conducting unauthorized experiments during laparoscopic procedures, leaving his initial, the letter J, marked with a cautery inside the abdominal cavity. This behavior led to him being labeled a psychopath. His fascination with procuring organs from still-living patients marked him as an expert in precise surgical cuts to preserve organs for transplantation.

Julio harbored a distorted perspective in his mind that drove him to heal his patients through precise incisions. He possessed exceptional skill with the scalpel and, like a virtuoso of art in the world of video games, demonstrated innate dexterity with laparoscopic sticks. However, his major problem lay in his inclination to resolve any situation by resorting to the scalpel, even when the patient did not suffer from the treated ailment. When removing the gallbladder, for example, he ventured to remove the appendix without justification, and if he found any anomaly in the liver or spleen, he dared to excise a segment under the premise of a necessary biopsy. Although he lacked the necessary consent and skill for such interventions, Julio was not concerned in the slightest. On numerous occasions during his fourth year of surgery, when his supervisor was not present in the operating room, he was allowed to act freely given his recognized surgical skill. The operating room staff considered him eccentric due to his constant jokes, some more macabre than others. What they did not know was that Julio kept a precise record of each of his acts on this sinister journey.

Rosalinda, a nurse graduated from the same hospital where Julio was doing his residency, shared a childless marriage with him. After facing difficulties in conceiving, they discovered that both were sterile due to problems with Rosalinda's ovaries and the lack of spermatogonia in Julio's testicles. This news, added to Julio's dismissal as a resident, triggered a deep depression in him and a growing resentment towards the system. The need for revenge became his motivation.

After his dismissal, Julio faced considerable difficulties in finding employment. Working in a bar or as an assistant in a grocery store were not options that satisfied him; his longing was to return to the operating room to explore human anatomy. Making precise cuts with the scalpel, removing the piece with an innate skill as when he was a surgical resident. Julio's lack of employment generated a financial imbalance in the couple, as Rosalinda's salary was not enough to cover their joint expenses. While Julio spent more time on the street, he ended up meeting Papote, a local drug trafficker with connections in the underworld, including human trafficking and the procurement of organs for sale and transplant. Papote could receive up to thirty thousand dollars for an adult kidney, but the price increased to fifty thousand dollars if it was a newborn's kidney.

Papote, a Mexican deported from his country for leading a criminal life, was dedicated to organ trafficking, such as lungs, hearts, and kidneys. In addition to his illegal activities, he had peculiar culinary preferences, as he enjoyed tasting organs of animals that most would avoid. Among his choices were brain matter, thyroid, kidneys, and testicles. He was an abominable consumer of any animal that moved on two legs or crawled. His cannibalism dated back a decade when, during a deplorable initiation into a fraternity characterized by kidnappings and human trafficking, especially of young people aged thirteen to fifteen, his companions introduced human flesh into his mouth with his eyes blindfolded. Since discovering that the delicious delicacy was the ribs of a modern human being, he had no qualms about continuing his culinary expedition devouring other fragments of the organism. He was fascinated by sautéed thyroid with plenty of caramelized onion and enjoyed frozen brains in red fruit syrup, convinced that the more brains he consumed, the more intelligent he would become.

Papote moved with the cunning of a snake, capable of executing a kidnapping without hesitation. Sometimes, he resorted to gaseous sedatives to put his victims to sleep, avoiding their screams and resistance. He paid known drug addicts generously to dispose of the kidnapped bodies, as he rarely returned the victims alive. Immersed in constant drug use, Papote made small errors in his misdeeds, which, with the acumen of a skilled detective, could have been obvious. Fortunately, his good luck persisted in his dark trade, as the drug addicts would not betray him since Papote was their regular provider of drug money.

Under the dark influence of Papote, the young Melquiades became an instrument for his latest atrocity. Disguised behind a dense beard, he was made unrecognizable and, in exchange for doses of pure cocaine, was entrusted to pose as a vegetable seller. His task was to deliver an elixir prepared with coconut water to a young couple in the Caguana neighborhood, plunging them into a lethargic state with powerful barbiturates, and then steal their newborn. In the shadows of the night, Papote would stealthily enter the room where the three rested, wrapped in a baby blanket, taking with him the last offspring born in that humble dwelling.

Once with the little one in his arms, Papote would dispose of the only living evidence. He would offer Melquiades a dose of cocaine adulterated with talcum and potent amphetamines, sealing his fate with the Lord. The fatality was fulfilled when, two days after the kidnapping, Melquiades was found livid, pale, with a strangely happy expression, but without a heartbeat. The details of the autopsy revealed intoxication by sympathomimetics, probably associated with a massive myocardial infarction. The corpse remained in the morgue for forty-five days without being claimed until the forensic institute proceeded as stipulated by law.

Rosalinda experienced profound disillusionment when facing Julio's academic debacle, who was expelled like a disposable bag from the surgical residency program. Despite knowing Julio's impulsiveness, she had always perceived in him an affable character, at least in his treatment of her. Rosalinda came from a family environment marked by the tyrannical authority of her father, who used to mistreat her mother in front of her. The dominant figure of Don Pedro gradually turned the two only women in his life submissive. Rosalinda's mother, Doña Rosa, was a woman of strong character, always immersed in reading two or three books a week, while Don Pedro ran a property sales and rental agency near their home.

After midday, Don Pedro stealthily retired to his abode to enjoy one or two whiskies with coconut, thus preparing his spirits for what would come later, as they say, to "open the vein." Despite having graduated from a private school, Rosalinda could only complete a bachelor's degree in nursing and began working at the early age of eighteen. Her love for children led her to take charge of the pediatric area and the newborn room at the hospital. She knew everything related to this short age of life. She couldn't have children, but she consoled herself by caring for the sick children of others.

Julio, sporadically, brought home a newborn baby, claiming that it was an orphan and that they were temporary parents on behalf of a secret society for which he worked. Despite Rosalinda's persistent questions about the origin of these children, Julio's answers were so vague that the trust between them was strengthened. Given their economic situation, adopting a baby was impossible, but the secret society provided food and items for the crib, thus facilitating temporary care. Julio took care of the baby during the day while Rosalinda worked, and she enjoyed the little one for the rest of the day. The presence of these children in Julio and Rosalinda's life was ephemeral. Every so often, a beautiful baby arrived who eventually disappeared from their lives, leaving an irreplaceable void.

In the house rented by Julio and Rosalinda on the outskirts of the city, there was an attic and a basement. Rosalinda had turned the attic into her oil painting space, while Julio used the basement as a sort of operating room to continue practicing surgery in case the remote opportunity to re-enter a medical residency program arose. Julio meticulously outfitted the place with a large refrigerator intended to store dry ice and human remains. The operating table was rescued from the last renovation of a bankrupt hospital that was getting rid of it. He incorporated powerful ceiling bulbs with light-emitting diodes to illuminate his procedures and gradually acquired surgical instruments economically through online platforms like eBay. He felt no need to sterilize the instruments since infections were a minor concern for those destined to lose all contact with the reality of life. He also had a tank of nitrous oxide that he used to sedate his prey, whether animals or humans. A rudimentary oximeter with an electrocardiogram completed his work storage. Occasionally, he asked Rosalinda, under the pretext of granting her an intimate session in bed, to bring him sterile scalpels of different sizes. His fascination with carrying out pseudo-experiments had expanded from stray dogs and homeless people to include newborns provided by the mysterious secret society for their temporary care.

3

On the sinister morning of May 7th of this fateful year, Juan Eduardo and Marta faced the grim reality of a home now orphaned. After three weeks of care and affection for their firstborn, Isabel, whom they fed diligently, they were plunged into horror when they discovered that their little one had mysteriously disappeared from their dwelling at ten in the morning. At that crucial moment, both Juan Eduardo and Marta lay in a deep sleep, unaware of the dark fate lurking in the shadows.

In the eerie village of the Jurutungo neighborhood in Jayuya, the couple resided in a humble two-bedroom, one-bathroom house with a living-dining room and kitchen, spanning about 250 square meters. Electricity, when the capricious company allowed, lit up the house amid dense vegetation, where imposing Meaito trees stood out, constituting almost a third of the island's forest cover. The house was Marta's family inheritance, serving as her grandmother's home and where she herself had grown up.

Just two years ago, Juan Eduardo and Marta had sealed their marital union. Juan Eduardo worked as an unassociated grain collector in the coffee fields of Yauco, earning a meager pay of six dollars per hour for hard work in the plantation or harvest. A small sum that increased by half a peso if it included packaging and preparation. Despite this nearly enslaving salary, small additions to daily life reached the couple's modest dwelling.

In their second year of marriage, Juan Eduardo and Marta eagerly awaited the arrival of their firstborn, whose gender they had discovered through prenatal ultrasound. The expected date of birth was set for the end of April. However, Marta, like every first-time and nervous mother, surprised everyone by going into labor two weeks early, breaking waters in mid-April. On April 14th, Isabel emerged, a beautiful creature weighing five pounds and six ounces, whose cry echoed powerfully in the gloomy environment surrounding the dwelling.

In his daily routine, Juan Eduardo usually left home at four thirty in the morning to go to Yauco on public transport. He depended on two public vehicles and the benevolence of any driver who might offer him a ride upon recognizing him walking to the public stop. However, on the fateful morning of May 7th, Juan Eduardo chose not to go to work. Instead, he lay in deep sleep next to Marta, waking up around ten in the morning to discover that little Isabel was no longer present by their side.

After receiving a distressing emergency call, the police's kidnapping unit arrived at the scene, accompanied by federal agents who maintained a distant presence in the investigation. They interrogated the young couple, submerged in despair over their loss, posing a series of probing questions. Inquiries were made about possible extramarital relationships that could have triggered the fury of a vengeful partner, details about compromising places were explored, questions were asked about whether they had received threats from anyone, and illicit drug use was inquired about.

The truth was that the day before, the couple had visited the market square of the town of Jayuya to buy groceries and chicken meat. During the shopping process, a street vendor insisted they try a natural passion fruit juice, which they ended up buying after tasting the peculiar concoction. On the night of May 6th, they consumed more than half of the bottle, falling into a daze and a deep sleep that lasted for more than fourteen hours.

Agent Meléndez, belonging to the division of crimes associated with kidnappings, meticulously recorded the information provided by the couple the day after the abduction of their baby. Following the same protocol that Darío applied in the case of the first infant crime, he urged the couple to undergo doping tests at the forensic laboratory to determine if they had been exposed to any toxic substances. While the interrogation focused on the physical characteristics of little Isabel to create a profile that could identify her in case she appeared, Marta shared with the agent crucial anatomical details, highlighting the peculiarity that the two fingers of the girl's right hand were joined; specifically, the middle and ring fingers, a condition known as syndactyly.

Two weeks later, while the baby remained missing and without any evident trace of her kidnappers, the test results revealed abnormal levels in the blood of both parents, indicating the presence of a barbiturate substance called sodium thiopental (Pentothal).

As the wait for news from the kidnappers plunged everyone into a chill of anxiety, Agent Meléndez incorporated the relevant details of the kidnapping into the electronic register of the command post. He desperately sought connections, investigating whether similar events had taken place in other parts of the island. The clues in this case were scarce, limited to the vendor in the market square, who was emerging as a figure of interest and required to be interviewed. Just half an hour after entering the information, Darío called the precinct where Meléndez was, sharing the ominous details of the first crime and highlighting the lack of additional information about the modus operandi of the kidnappers or abductors of newborns.

In truth, neither the vegetable seller involved in the first case nor the street vendor from the market square had been identified, despite the current couple having provided a pencil sketch as part of their advice for the investigation. The mystery surrounding the perpetrators remained, extending its shadow over both cases.

The federal agents involved in the kidnapping case were limited by the scant evidence available, which included the two sketches of individuals of interest. Using facial recognition methods, they identified two different people matching the portraits drawn by police artists. In both instances, the suspects turned out to be drug addicts with criminal records associated with habitual substance abuse. Interestingly, both individuals had died from drug overdoses, and their bodies had been abandoned at the Forensic Institute's morgue, awaiting a relative to claim them. In both cases, the lack of relatives or friends to recognize them and provide a proper burial led to the application of the law allowing for the disposal of the bodies. The sinister connection between the kidnappers and their tragic fates raised disconcerting questions in the dark progress of the investigation.

After thirty-five days of anguished uncertainty since Isabel's disappearance, a macabre discovery plunged the community into unspeakable terror. The decomposed body of an infant was ominously and statically discovered floating in the Caricaboa River. This river, capable of generating a dangerous current when the rains unleashed, dragged along everything in its course. A group of young people enjoying a swim in the river's waters witnessed the horrifying discovery: a body wrapped in a black plastic bag floated adrift. They immediately alerted the authorities, moving the bag to the shore.

Law enforcement took charge of the scene, arranging for the bag and the body to be transported to the forensic institute in search of answers. The macabre truth emerged: it was a baby girl of about a month and a half old, the victim of a meticulous cut that went from the chin to the pubic symphysis. The neck, chest, and abdomen, including the retroperitoneum, were empty of their usual organs, extracted with impressive precision, as if they were destined to be replaced by themselves. The eye sockets were missing. Although facial decomposition made it difficult to identify the baby, the autopsy revealed a significant detail: in her right hand, the ring finger was joined to the middle finger by syndactyly, a detail that intensified the dark nature of the horror that had enveloped the little one.

Interestingly, in the left corner of the interior of the abdominal cavity, a cautery tool had been used to etch what appeared to be a letter, possibly the letter "J", encircled by three dots.

The Forensic Institute communicated with state and federal authorities via an email that included photographs of the horrendous crime committed. At the command post, the news was received with relative calm until the mention of the joined fingers on the right hand of the baby. Faced with this shocking detail, Agent Meléndez immediately contacted Juan Eduardo and Marta, bringing them to the forensic institute to assist in the investigation of this atrocious murder.

Upon seeing the right hand of their daughter Isabel, Marta collapsed, victim to a vasovagal syncope. The couple painfully identified the mutilated child as their own daughter, proceeding to sign the necessary documents and taking the small body to provide a Christian burial.

"Marta, do you think we will ever find justice for our little Isabel?" Juan Eduardo asked.

"I don't know, Juan Eduardo. I just wish those responsible pay for what they did to our daughter," Marta replied.

After burying Isabel, the couple sank into a depression that endured throughout their lives. They never managed to overcome the devastating impact caused by the tragedy.

The case was filed as an unsolved enigma in the records of the state command and in the files of the federal authorities, who began to outline a pattern behind the abductions. The scapegoat, who supplied the pentothal in liquid form, was an addict with a criminal history, whose death by overdose seemed to be a constant. However, something more sinister was at play; someone or several individuals were manipulating this population of drug addicts, taking advantage of their vulnerability to fulfill their dark purposes.

The surgical precision of the autopsies performed on the victims, as if they were being prepared for a clandestine organ transplant, added an additional layer of mystery to the case. The mark in the form of an ellipse surrounding a "J" on the abdomens of the infants remained suspended in the air, leaving a sense of mystery and bewilderment. It was evident that the investigation needed to be transferred to the special section in charge of crimes related to the illegal sale of organs. A dark and dangerous world was opening up before the investigators, where greed and depravity intertwined in a web of intrigue and corruption.

A puzzle that baffled the authorities was the short viability of these organs, which required transplantation within a very limited time period. Considering the possibility that they might leave the island, it was deduced that the final destination had to be a country specializing in this sinister business, suggesting the need for short flights to ensure the freshness and effectiveness of the organs. The criminal plot took an even more intriguing turn, leading investigators down a path full of dangers and secrets hidden in the dark world of illegal organ sales.

4

As Rosalinda had grown fond of the first baby in February, whom she had to let go after a month, she also became attached to the beautiful three-week-old girl Julio brought home in May of that year. After four weeks, the newborn had to leave, as dictated by the secret society to which Julio belonged. Rosalinda noticed the small red strawberry on the left forearm of the first baby boy and the joined fingers on the right hand of the girl. She even consulted with a hand surgeon at the hospital where she worked, who indicated that the baby girl's fingers could be separated between six months and one year of age, without any rush. This information mysteriously alerted Julio, who reprimanded Rosalinda, warning her not to get her hopes up with the babies he temporarily brought to the residence, as they didn't have the financial resources to keep them for longer periods. Only enough time to cover the expenses provided by the society while the destinies of the infants were arranged.

Julio always warned Rosalinda in advance when it was time to return the baby to their future guardians, allowing her a brief period of farewell filled with the tenderness she was known for. Just as Rosalinda handled pediatric patients in her hospital wing with dedication, she provided loving and selfless care to the temporary little ones Julio brought home.

Unlike many, Rosalinda did not immerse herself in social networks or communication devices that brought and carried discouraging news of life. Her delight was to immerse herself in her own simple world, dedicating herself to the institution of pediatric care and returning home to accompany her troubled husband. Together, they worked to overcome the fear that plagued him, seeking to excel again in life. Beyond that, in her leisure moments, Rosalinda took refuge in the attic, sketching drawings that she later filled with the intensity of oil paint. However, behind the facade of tranquility, an aura of mystery began to tinge the walls of her peaceful home. Her pleasure was found in living in her simple world, dedicating herself to her work in childcare and being at home with her husband, with whom she struggled to overcome the fears that disturbed him and seek to stand out in life once more.

In that fateful year, the news spread through social networks with few comments and direct references, as the reason behind the organ extraction from the victims was unclear. Moreover, there was an avoidance of generating panic among young couples, fearful that there might be a serial killer trading in organs, especially with a predilection for newborns. State and federal authorities were mired in confusion about the case, depending on citizen collaboration to obtain specific details about the occurrence and nature of these atrocious crimes. Crimes that had already triggered the social destabilization of two couples who shared a deep love.

In Rosalinda's naive mind, the idea that Julio could be in any way linked to the disappearances of infants was unthinkable, too remote a concept for her perception of reality. However, a growing concern led her to confront her fears and address the issue directly with him. In a moment of courage mixed with anxiety, she approached Julio and asked him in a trembling but firm voice:

"Julio, what do you think about the disappearances of babies that are being discussed on social networks?"

Julio's reaction was immediate and disproportionate, almost theatrical in its intensity. With a forced laugh and a tone of mockery, he dismissed the idea as utter nonsense.

"That's just nonsense, Rosalinda! Inventions of those internet fanatics looking for attention. There's no truth in those stories circulating on the networks, just nonsense to get 'likes'," he exclaimed with vehemence that seemed to hide something deeper.

Rosalinda, though trying to convince herself that Julio was right, couldn't shake a persistent feeling of doubt. That excessive reaction, that marked disdain for a topic causing alarm in the community... something didn't fit. Julio's response, rather than calming her, only served to stir the waters of her unease further.

As the nights passed, Rosalinda found herself increasingly awake, contemplating the darkness, her mind spinning around a carousel of thoughts and suspicions she would have previously considered unthinkable. Each news about a new case of infant disappearance, each alert that appeared on her phone, became an echo that resonated in the silent hallways of her mind, fueling a growing storm of doubts and fears.

The situation reached a point where Rosalinda could no longer deny that something was terribly wrong. A part of her, the part that still wanted to believe in Julio's goodness, struggled to stay afloat in a sea of denial. But another part, a darker and more realistic part, began to accept that the truth might be much more terrifying than she had ever imagined.

While social media users reveled in their reggaeton idols, their full-body selfies, their sculptural and exotic bodies, as well as the details of their latest dinners and the sensational wine they consumed, they preferred to ignore the tragic reality that was unfolding. Love itself, when overcultivated, could turn out to be harmful, especially when society was so immersed in its superficial pleasures as to face the harsh reality of such a heart-wrenching situation. The widespread indifference threatened to obscure the truth, plunging society into a whirlpool of ignorance and self-indulgence.

Julio and Papote had accumulated a small fortune thanks to the sale of internal organs of newborns. Their earnings far exceeded what Julio would have earned if he had pursued a conventional career as a transplant surgeon. Essentially, both had established a lucrative internal and external business centered on the sale of organs from newborns and infants. Julio handled the extraction and preservation of the organs, while Papote managed the distribution both in the local black market and abroad. They had a plane that made trips of less than two hours to transport the necessary organs to their destination. Everything operated like a mafia, both in the country of origin and at the destination of the organs, where they were immediately transplanted.

Using an encrypted program exclusively manipulated by Julio or Papote, information about the organs destined for trade was transmitted beforehand to a clandestine network, with a suggested price and in a completely undetectable manner, immune to any hacking attempt. Crucial details such as the age and gender of the involuntary donor, blood type, and suggested price were specified. Once the fund transfer was made to a Swiss account, the extraction date was set to ensure that the recipients were ready in the operating room, prepared to receive the frozen organ packed in a sealed and sterile container. The only documentation sent included the gender, age of the patient, and time of extraction. After the delivery of the organ, the aircraft returned to its point of origin. Increasingly, the organs remained on the island, safeguarded in a clandestine laboratory, where clandestine recipients were prepared to receive and implant them. The number of clandestine transplants in the area increased as the need of the sick population grew, despite having very limited financial resources to carry out the procedure.

As time went by, Julio and Papote watched their profits grow with the prosperous organ trade. Their mafia structure was impeccable; the organs reached their destinations in perfect condition and with precise surgical cuts.

In another room, Julio spoke in a low voice on the phone. "Yes, everything is ready," he said tensely. "The extraction will be tomorrow, make sure the container is prepared." He hung up and remained silent for a moment, wrestling with his thoughts.

This ensured successful transplants for the recipients, restoring their health and happiness. Individuals with resistant diabetes, uncontrolled alcoholism, and unmanaged hypertension benefited from receiving new kidneys, livers, and hearts, gradually freeing them from the usual burdens of life that seemed insurmountable. These recipients were not ordinary individuals; they were those immersed in the dark world of crime who needed to postpone their miseries a bit longer. Corneas allowed unrestricted vision of that underworld. Payments for the orders and donations of these organs were generous, giving recipients the opportunity to start anew with organs as young as theirs. Additionally, the possibility of immunological rejection was lower, as these organs were developing with stem cells. Using the donors' blood, the pseudo-doctors created chimeras in the recipients to avoid organ rejection, eliminating the need for immunosuppression therapies. The only thing missing was establishing an organ clone farm to eradicate rejection once and for all.

In October of that year, with no end in sight, Rosalinda received the exciting news that another baby was on the way. It was a little boy, just three weeks old. On October 1st, Julio and Rosalinda's residence was once again filled with the melodious sounds and soft cries of a beautiful newborn. Since Rosalinda was well-prepared, she had no need to buy diapers, only fresh formula to feed her new temporary stepson.

While cradling little Juancito, Rosalinda whispered tenderly, "Little one, every moment with you is a gift, even if brief." Her voice was a soft whisper, full of love and sadness.

The tale of orphanhood that surrounded the little ones who arrived at her home kept Rosalinda oblivious to the harsh reality. Her only desire was to provide ephemeral affection and love to the baby affected by the absence of his parents.

On the same day, October 1st, Juancito, as his young parents named him, was a victim of a kidnapping in the Garzas neighborhood of Adjuntas. Garzas is located in the mountainous region of central Puerto Rico, in the foothills of the Central Mountain Range. Amidst hills, lush vegetation, and a mountain climate, stood the modest dwelling of Pablo and Teresa. Juancito, their firstborn, was conceived with considerable difficulty, as the couple spent over fifteen thousand dollars on modern assisted reproduction techniques. Given Teresa's lack of a uterus, they turned to her sister Carmen as a surrogate. Carmen, a single lawyer with a difficult temperament, always scrutinized every corner of her surroundings and did not tolerate being kept in the dark. She was willing to fight to the end to achieve her goals, whatever they might be. She was a tough nut to crack. Without Carmen's cooperation, this case would never have been conclusively and definitively resolved.

Meanwhile, in Pablo and Teresa's house, a heartbreaking dialogue took place:

Teresa, with tears in her eyes, asked, "How could this happen, Pablo? How was Juancito so cruelly snatched from us?"

Pablo, embracing her, replied with a broken voice, "I don't know, my love. But I promise we'll do everything we can to find him. I won't rest until our son is back home."

Meanwhile, Carmen, in her office, spoke on the phone with determination: "Listen, I need you to check every security camera in the Garzas area. Something doesn't fit here. I'm sure there's something we're overlooking."

5

On the morning of October 1st, Lieutenant
Santiago, stationed at the Adjuntas town
police station, received notification of a
possible kidnapping of a minor in the
mountainous region known as the Garzas
neighborhood. He turned to his men and
said, "Quick, we need to go to Garzas
neighborhood..." He dispatched two of his
officers to the scene, a modest one-room
dwelling that was the epicenter of the
problem. There, Pablo and Teresa, a young
couple, mourned the disappearance of their
three-week-old newborn, which occurred in
the early hours of that day. Like the previous
parents, Pablo and Teresa had slept through
the night, leaving the newborn unattended.

Carmen, Teresa's sister who had served as a
surrogate for Juancito, the missing baby, also
arrived at the scene. Teresa, in tears, said,
"Sister, I don't know how this could have
happened..."

According to the investigation, the day
before, Pablo and Teresa were visited by a
vegetable vendor who offered them an elixir
that supposedly would help the couple cope

with sleep. Juancito, being an active and insatiable baby, demanded to be breastfed every two hours. After Teresa's last feeding, the couple consumed the concocted spoonful of the elixir and fell into a deep state of drowsiness, waking up at eight in the morning the next day. Upon awakening, they discovered that the crib was empty, and the familiar cooing of the little bird sound had disappeared.

The primary suspect emerged as Carmen, the surrogate mother. She had a solid alibi, as she lived with her mother, who confirmed her alibi. A sketch of the elixir seller was generated, and samples of it were taken for toxicological tests. A detailed report was prepared and presented to the local police kidnapping section, and the federal authorities resumed the investigation, collecting relevant evidence in the case. The report was distributed to all police stations in the country, including Jayuya and Utuado, where a similar kidnapping had been reported at the beginning of the year. Technically, it could not be classified as a kidnapping, as no ransom was requested, and no one claimed responsibility for the incidents, but it was the third case of a newborn abduction. The two previous cases had resulted in the discovery of the babies mutilated and without organs.

The toxicological test of the elixir showed a positive result for a significant amount of barbiturates, enough to sedate a considerable group of animals. The baby was found approximately a month and a half later, inside a black plastic bag on the shore of the Río Grande de Adjuntas, with an autopsy report indicating his death two weeks prior. Like in the previous cases, he had the characteristic incision from the chin to the pubic symphysis, displaying a body without internal organs and precise surgical cuts. Equine thread was used to close the skin, making an impeccable seam. Whoever perpetrated this act demonstrated exceptional surgical skills. In the left corner of the inside of the abdominal cavity, what appeared to be a letter, possibly the letter "J," surrounded by three points, had been etched.

The identification of Juancito's body occurred when his parents, Pablo, and Carmen, recognized the distinctive light brown mole on the deceased's back. The shocking news plunged the couple into a state of shock from which they never fully recovered. This cruel and undeserved blow profoundly altered their lives.

Carmen, the lawyer, was overwhelmed by disbelief. She couldn't fathom that her careless sister had allowed the baby to be abducted. She delved into the two previous cases, visiting federal facilities in search of help and information about possible culprits. What concrete information did she have? All cases involved newborns under thirty days old, the couples only had one child, and lived in remote places on the island, a pattern emerged in central Puerto Rico affecting Jayuya, Utuado, and now Adjuntas. In all incidents, someone sold the couples some food that left them unconscious; there was no violence at the scene of the abduction, no one communicated or assumed responsibility, and two of the babies appeared mutilated and empty. Additionally, in the two previous cases, the individuals from the sketches had criminal records as drug users, found dead with unclaimed bodies at the forensic morgue. Carmen was intrigued by the reason behind the extraction of internal organs. Although the answer seemed obvious, the lawyer's mind could not conceive of such abomination of human organ sales, much less at such a tender age. Who in their right mind could commit such atrocious crimes?...

The lawyer Carmen visited the forensic institute determined to discuss the autopsy results of Juancito and gather more information about previous cases. However, she faced limitations in the information the forensic team could provide to a private individual. Her interest piqued, Carmen decided to interview agents Darío and Meléndez, who were available in nearby towns.

During her conversation with the forensic pathologists, Carmen inquired about the purpose of the precise cuts in the organ extraction. The pathologist suggested the possibility of a psychopath with surgical skills or organ trafficking as the main motivation due to the significant financial benefit derived from such macabre activities.

Darío, Meléndez, and Carmen met at a café in Utuado to discuss the situation. "Do you see the pattern here? All these cases have to be connected," Carmen expressed. They all shared perplexity at the events and vividly remembered the previous cases. After thorough discussion, they concluded that child organ trafficking was the main reason behind the crimes and decided to look for a leading gang involved in these dark dealings. They were seeking a macabre mind that also had surgical skills. Unbeknownst to them, some organs were exported out of the country, while others stayed to meet the demands of the local underworld.

The key lay in the drug consumers in the neighborhood where Julio and Rosalinda lived. A group of wandering individuals used an abandoned house as a refuge, indulging in all kinds of poisons, especially ecstasy. Papote occasionally recruited some of them to act as sellers, thus facilitating the sedation of the couples of the newborns he planned to kidnap for organ trafficking. He then administered an amplified dose of the drug, and these actors died from an overdose of their own poison. This way, he abruptly broke the chain of events linking him to the crime, avoiding investigation.

Papote's problem arose when he failed to induce the last drug addict to death, the one used to sedate Juancito's parents. The drug he administered was not potent enough to end the individual's life. This last one ended up in the hospital, where they revived him through hemodialysis. However, this caused acute renal failure in the drug addict, keeping him connected to a machine for three weeks. This witness was the only one capable of contradicting Papote and Julio, revealing part of the scheme behind the kidnappings. Both were unaware that the drug addict had not died.

The story of Rolando, the addict who survived Julio and Papote's malicious plans, is astonishing to tell. Over time, Rolando became a successful banker and trader, living an enviable life with his beautiful wife. However, a tragic car accident took his beloved's life, leaving her unrecognizable due to severe injuries. The body was irreparable, transformed into an indistinguishable mass of flesh, bones, viscera, and skin, submerged in a pool of dark blood. Seeking a solution to his pain, Rolando delved into the world of extrasensory fantasies and telekinesis, consulting as many spiritual mediums as he could find. He paid a fortune to a supposed magician who claimed he could resurrect his wife. With a spell involving his beloved's hair and various internal garments, the magician managed to induce some movement in the grave. This prompted him to request the exhumation of the corpse, only to face the horrific amalgam of intertwined and rotten organs, causing him an insurmountable trauma. He abandoned his banking career, his life, becoming one more wanderer, surrendering to constant drug and narcotic use.

Rolando, the sole survivor, and subject of interest matching the sketch provided by Pablo and Teresa to the police graphic artist during their mourning, required an interview. Federal agents headed to the hospital where Rolando was admitted, accompanied by law enforcement officers. The visit was uncomfortable for Rolando, who was under the influence of potent sedatives following his medical resurrection. They asked him about selling a sleep-fighting elixir to the young couple, Pablo, and Teresa, but he didn't remember that detail. He only pointed out that Teresa seemed tired due to a prolonged childbirth. He didn't recall helping the couple, as Teresa needed rest due to anemia, as mentioned by Julio. However, Rolando was unaware of the details. He knew that if he followed Julio and Papote's simple instructions, he would enjoy ecstasy mixed with fentanyl, leading him to experience divine lights in the sky, recalling his mutilated wife.

After the fruitless interaction with law enforcement, Rolando, more out of fear than difficulty, inquired about the reason why he had become a target of investigation by the authorities. He was increasingly anxious trying to understand why both local police and federal agents were showing interest in him. When the agents revealed that he was identified in a sketch as the individual who had provided a sedative to Pablo and Teresa, whose child was abducted and mutilated to death, Rolando was horrified. He wondered who, in their right mind, could be committing such heinous crimes. He knew that once he recovered, he would have to undergo a lineup so that Juancito's parents could verify whether the person in the sketch was really him or not.

After the tense conversation with the agents, Rolando was even more disturbed. His mind clouded by sedatives; his trembling voice broke the silence of the hospital room.

"Who could do something like this?" he murmured; his gaze lost in the emptiness of the room. "I don't know anything about sedatives or kidnappings... I just wanted to help Teresa, she... she was suffering so much..."

A law enforcement officer interrupted, his cold tone resonating in the sterile room. "We're not here to hear excuses. We're here to find answers. And if you're guilty, you'll pay for your actions."

Rolando felt a chill run down his spine. "But I did nothing! I swear on my deceased wife, on what I hold dearest in this world!"

The agents exchanged skeptical glances. "We'll see when you recover. Then, you'll have the chance to prove your innocence... or face the consequences," they warned, before leaving Rolando submerged in a sea of doubts and terror.

6

Julio, plagued by deep unease, muttered to himself, "Did Rolando survive that lethal mix? I need to make sure before continuing..." The trail of Rolando had vanished after the attempted murder by administering a cocaine overdose mixed with generous doses of fentanyl. The uncertainty of whether Rolando had succumbed to the deadly mixture tormented him. It was imperative to verify this crucial detail before continuing with his illicit activities.

He repeatedly scoured the dark corners of the drug addicts' commune, the stage he used for his schemes. Approaching an acquaintance, he cautiously asked, "Have you seen or heard anything about Rolando lately?" None of his sources could provide information about Rolando's fate. With cunning, he left messages with other victims he knew, alert to the possibility that Rolando might emerge. He knew there was always someone willing to talk for money or drugs.

Eventually, news reached him: his prey was admitted to the Municipal Hospital of the

Mountain, just fifteen minutes from his residence. It did not escape his notice that this was the same center where Rosalinda worked. Additional information revealed that Rolando was listed as a person of interest, linked to a portrait made by Juancito's parents. This was a delicate matter; he had to eliminate Rolando to avoid the consequences of being exposed and facing prison, a prospect he deemed inevitable for the supposed good he believed he was doing.

Julio was plagued with ominous certainties. He suffered from impostor syndrome, convincing himself that he was a skilled transplant surgeon who never had the opportunity to stand out. He refused to recognize his status as a fake doctor, never validating his general medicine license or surgical specialist license due to his aggressive, reckless, and authoritarian temperament.

Paradoxically, he showed a completely different side to Rosalinda. Despite his professional deceptions, both shared the disillusionment of not being able to conceive children in their previous marriages. Instead, they found temporary comfort in briefly caring for newborns destined to suffer the relentless precision of his scalpel.

Julio, with loving guile, extracted information from Rosalinda about the neonates born at the Mountain Hospital. This time, he needed to access Rolando's room to eliminate this link in his chain of misdeeds once and for all. He feared that Rosalinda would connect the cases of the missing babies with his own criminal acts.

The plan was to disguise himself as a doctor to enter Rolando's room, he told himself while looking in the mirror. Preferably at night and administer an insulin injection. This would cause a drop in blood sugar that would be fatal to the neurons. Insulin, easily accessible without a license, would be obtained from the crash cart, located in every corner of the hospitals.

However, fate, always unpredictable, was about to alter the course of his schemes.

Confined to the third floor of the institution, specifically in the internal medicine area, Rolando was experiencing a notable recovery from the overdose, though he remained oblivious to the reason for his hospital admission. To counteract the adverse effects of previous substances, he was administered potent sedatives and tranquilizers, plunging him into a deep sleep for most of the day and night. Unbeknownst to him, far from his understanding, Julio was planning a visit to conclude what had been left pending.

Clad in a white coat, wearing fake credentials, and even a stethoscope swinging around his neck, Julio stealthily made his way to Rolando's room the day after gathering details about the events. In the utility room, he found a crash cart and three vials of insulin. Approaching the nearly deceased Rolando, he used the accessory port of the venous line to inject a full vial, inducing a gradual descent.

At that moment, Rolando, seemingly having more lives than a cat, opened his eyes and saw his drug supplier friend manipulating his IV. Gradually, Rolando experienced pallor, cold sweats, and motor weakness, beginning a descent into unconsciousness, as if entering a tunnel. His heart rate spiked, alerting the monitor at the nurses' station. Alarms sounded both on the machine at the station and in the room's electrocardiogram.

Realizing the situation, Julio hastily left the room. At that moment, the on-duty nurse entered, noticing the recent presence of a doctor leaving the room. After checking Rolando's vital signs and performing a blood sugar test with a finger prick, she discovered his blood sugar level was a concerning 15 mg%. Acting swiftly, she opened the crash cart and injected a hypertonic sugar solution. Rolando, for the second time in his life, revived.

The nurse, alerted by the situation, contacted the police, and reported her observations, mentioning the unauthorized administration of insulin. She conducted tests for insulin levels in the blood to support her findings. The police decided to place surveillance on the person of interest. Routine inquiries focused on identifying the man in the coat who left the room seconds after the cardiac monitors' alarms activated. Although they couldn't see his face, they planned to review the hallway's video recordings to unravel the suspect's identity.

The room lacked surveillance cameras; these were only in the hallways and nursing stations.

Once again, luck smiled on Julio. The surveillance cameras captured only the rear silhouette of a man about six feet tall, with dark hair. No beard was visible, but since he didn't face the camera, it was difficult to confirm this detail. Upon leaving the room, instead of heading to the nursing station, he took a detour to the institution's emergency exit. He descended the stairs to the first floor, discarded the coat, and quickly got into his black Toyota, eager to leave the place as soon as possible. Once more, frustration enveloped him for failing to eliminate Rolando.

It was imperative to keep a low profile while figuring out the next move. Dealing with Rolando would no longer be so straightforward, given that he was under local police surveillance.

Upon returning home, Rosalinda was already there, having prepared dinner. Julio, displaying anxiety, was questioned by Rosalinda about the cause of his disturbance. "What's wrong, Julio? You seem worried," Rosalinda asked. Julio, disguising his nervousness, replied, "Just frustrations from work, nothing important..." His beloved's heart ached with the lament of her life. He tasted a bite of the dinner Rosalinda had prepared before retiring to his secret sanctuary: the meticulously constructed operating room in the basement of their home. A haven where, with innate precision, he performed the delicate task of extracting the organs he needed for his commercial transactions, all those already waiting on a clandestine list. It was in this clandestine space, among shadows and surgical whispers, that he wove his web of medical crimes with surgical skill and calculated coldness.

In each of Julio's merciless acts, the majesty of his coldness was manifested in a macabre setting. His skill was encapsulated in the art of sedating the newborn into a deep sleep that did not bring immediate death. This method allowed him to extract certain organs before others, minimizing the recovery time before being transported and reimplanted into other recipients.

The ritual began with a precise incision from the chin to the pubic symphysis, executed with a cautery pen easily acquired on the eBay platform for about $412. Without concern for infections, he sterilized the tool by immersing it in a Cidex disinfectant solution that he never bothered to change. After removing the eyeballs, in the neck, he extracted the thyroid, storing it in the refrigerator as a succulent appetizer that his partner Papote enjoyed with delight. Papote held the absurd belief that consuming thyroid improved his vitality.

Julio then discarded the trachea and cervical esophagus, considering them useless for his purposes. He focused his attention on the abdomen instead of the thorax, extracting the liver, small intestine, pancreas, and duodenum, while discarding the spleen and large intestine. He approached the retroperitoneum with the precision of a urological surgeon to remove the kidneys, cutting off circulation while removing the organs attached to the aorta and inferior vena cava. This allowed the future recipient to have ends to tie the renal vein and artery, along with the ureter that drains urine.

The bladder remained intact, though its notoriety led some people to request it to expand stomachs in patients who had lost theirs due to malignancies. Julio sent the liver attached to the duodenum and pancreas, using the circulation of the superior vena cava and the aorta near the kidneys.

The last organ to be removed, after the lungs, was the heart, with a shorter ischemia time and a considerable financial reward. At this stage, the baby's brain was deprived of blood flow, reaching a technical state of death. It was arduous work that took several hours, but the financial compensation was masterful. He always signed his works with the first initial of his name between three points.

Julio did not allow himself to resort to such vile methods as using acids to dissolve the bodies, as he lacked the heart necessary to commit such an atrocity and disfigure the skin of the one he had cared for. Instead, he placed the empty shell of the newborn in a black garbage bag and threw it into the nearest river to the place where he had carried out the abduction. This was yet another mistake that would eventually cost him in terms of his freedom.

7

The nurse who witnessed the insulin-assisted murder attempt on her patient had a past connection with Rosalinda; they had shared a training history at the nursing school. Despite their bonds, their professional careers led them in different directions within the institution. While Rosalinda worked on the second floor, specifically in the maternity and childcare area, her colleague worked on the third floor, focusing on internal medicine and adult care. She had gone through a complicated experience at work after discovering an individual disguised as a doctor trying to harm her addict patient. Their interactions were limited to occasional meetings in the cafeteria during coffee or lunch breaks. In their next encounter, she planned to reveal to Rosalinda that she lived in a world where appearances might be darker and more complex.

The police provided Rolando with protection after the attempted murder. They placed him in a safe house, albeit without constant surveillance. However, Rolando fell back into the grip of addiction, like any other consumer struggling with physical substance dependence. But his motivation went beyond that; he wanted to confront Julio, discover the reasons behind the murder attempt, and understand the connection with the missing and murdered babies.

Despite having experienced a nearly fatal hypoglycemia, which left several neurons, especially those of memory, inactive, Rolando claimed ignorance about the identity of the disguised doctor who tried to kill him when informing the police. Although he was fully aware of the truth, it was not yet the right time to reveal this crucial information. His recovery was gradual, but the anxiety generated by the drug prevented him from sleeping. He urgently needed a dose of narcotics to combat withdrawal syndrome. The need to contact Julio persisted, even if it meant risking his life for a third time.

Rosalinda met with the nurse affected by the attempted murder at the hospital three weeks later. "I can't get the image of that man in Rolando's room out of my head," the nurse confessed. "It was like he knew exactly what he was doing. The police provided protection for Rolando."

The nurse detailed her post-traumatic stress, revealing that the identity of the malicious doctor who tried to harm her patient was still unknown. However, she had knowledge about medications, as she had used insulin to reduce the patient's systemic glucose. She even showed Rosalinda a photo of the assailant taken from behind, extracted from the hospital's videos. Although not entirely sure, Rosalinda shuddered when, for a moment, she mistook the man in the photo for her husband from that perspective. Although Julio had been expelled from the surgery program and did not usually frequent the hospital, doubt lingered in Rosalinda's mind, who felt the need to confront Julio about this event.

As soon as she got home, Rosalinda used the intercom installed by Julio in the basement to call him and ask him to come up to the living room. "A nurse showed me a photo of a man at the hospital, and he looked a lot like you," Rosalinda said with a trembling voice. Julio, with forced calm, replied, "That's impossible, love. You must be confused."

Julio was busy preparing the surgical instruments, as a new intervention was approaching, and vital organs such as lungs, liver, and pancreas were needed for an underworld individual with severe respiratory and hepatic problems due to smoking and alcoholism. A drug lord who had enough money to buy several orders. Julio went up to the living room and greeted Rosalinda with a kiss. During the conversation, she shared the information provided by the nurse, pointing out that the man in the videos resembled him. Julio flatly denied being the person identified in the images and sowed doubts in Rosalinda's mind about his motives for attempting the life of an addict who had been admitted to the hospital for an overdose.

Rosalinda's significant alertness to Julio's comment raised serious doubts in her mind. "How did Julio know about Rolando's reason for admission?" she wondered to herself, feeling the doubt growing inside her. Although not known for her sharpness, Julio's revelation about Rolando's admission reason perplexed her. She had never discussed with Julio the exact reason for Rolando's admission, so it was disconcerting that he knew this privileged and confidential information about the patient's reason for admission.

Rosalinda couldn't link Rolando to Juancito's parents, as she avoided social media and remained aloof from even the most macabre news events, like the heart-wrenching disappearances and murders of newborns. Even though the nurse had updated her about these incidents, Rosalinda couldn't establish the connection between them due to her limited intellectual acuity to apply the law of associations. Julio, aware of Rosalinda's limited intellectual capacity, was deeply in love with her green eyes and imposing posterior. He didn't mind that Rosalinda suffered from polycystic ovary syndrome, which prevented her from conceiving. In the couple's fertility studies, it was revealed that Julio suffered from azoospermia, with a spermatocyte count close to zero. Together they faced the pain of an empty nest, which was only sporadically filled with the brief visits of the newborns that Julio brought to sacrifice.

Moreover, doubt began to sprout in Rosalinda's restricted mind. She questioned why her husband spent so much time in the basement, a place Julio had forbidden Rosalinda from the beginning. Doubts arose about the relationship between Julio and Rolando, as well as the fate of the three newborns who had spent the night in their home. Additionally, Rosalinda wondered how Julio obtained the money he claimed to have saved. It was necessary to pay more attention to the small details of life to connect the dots. Rosalinda felt the need to be more astute about her existence, knowing that this could trigger a grave and cruel, yet truthful revelation.

Detectives Darío and Meléndez, along with Carmen, headed to the hospital to interview the third-floor nurse, a witness to Rolando's murder attempt. "I'm sorry I can't provide more details," the nurse said, "but something about this case doesn't add up to me." They suspected there was a connection between this incident and the previous baby abductions.

Despite their efforts, the nurse did not reveal additional information to the agents and Carmen. Darío reviewed the records and discovered that Rolando was part of a key witness protection program and was incommunicado. The decision was made to follow Rolando, anticipating that, as a habitual drug user, he would eventually seek medication to satisfy his physical dependence. They would remain vigilant for any developments in the life of this witness, who curiously matched the profile that Pablo and Teresa had drafted based on the description of the vegetable seller.

8

"In November, the demand for thoracic and abdominal organs increased considerably... Prices are rising, Papote," Julio commented, "our efficiency must be impeccable now more than ever."

The encrypted request system continued to elevate the costs associated with this urgent need. Astutely, Julio employed artificial intelligence to access the organ request program, which he called "Ellipsis." This tool used a sequence of three dots as a response key for requests from those desperate for a transplant. Each set of dots indicated different levels of information: confirmation that the process was underway, the estimated date for the organ's availability, and the notification that the donor's internal parts were being extracted, respectively.

Papote was in charge of organizing the delivery for the Ellipsis society, informing the carriers and the on-duty pilot. Everything was part of an operation coordinated synchronously to minimize the ischemia time of the organs destined for distribution. A single body could generate up to half a million dollars, and after covering transportation costs, about a quarter million was left as net profit. The Ellipsis society did not assume responsibility for rejection issues or logistics in transplants; its role was limited to obtaining and harvesting organs from the youngest available innocent victims.

In the mountainous area of the Toro Negro neighborhood in Ciales, a young newlywed couple had established their home. Victor, looking at Rosa while holding Rosita, said, "Our little Rosita has brought so much light to our life." Rosa, with a loving smile, replied, "She is our little miracle." This marriage welcomed a girl who was just three weeks old, named Rosita. Victor and Rosa were completely unaware of what awaited their newborn. Living far away and distant from everyday events in a modest home built with local wood. Given the limited availability of electricity, they installed a solar panel system with a battery that covered the home's energy needs. Victor, with his associate degree in electricity, was instrumental in creating this electrical generation in such a remote neighborhood.

The girl was born at the municipal mountain hospital on November 1st through vaginal delivery, and mother and daughter were discharged in good health two days later. Curiously, Rosalinda, who also acted as a nurse, had attended to the baby, and noticed a strand of hair lighter in color at the back of her head, similar to an albino mole. As part of her professional skill, she recorded these findings in the newborn's electronic file.

Following a pattern similar to previous cases, a traveling vegetable vendor sold them food and products the day before the next kidnapping. They consumed a local tamarind juice, bottled in a wine bottle with an old cork, which resulted in a deep sleep of more than fourteen hours. This period was enough for Papote to raid Victor and Rosa's modest home and take their little daughter. He handed the newborn to Julio, who, with the cradle in hand, headed to his home while waiting for Rosalinda. That morning, he called her and informed her about their new guest. "We have a little visitor," Julio said with a smile. Rosalinda, excited, replied, "Another opportunity to be a mother!" The news made Rosalinda smile as she realized she would again assume the role of a surrogate mother for a period of time.

What Julio didn't know was that Rolando was waiting for him upon arrival with the girl. He patiently waited for him to settle in the residence and then knocked on the door. Julio, seeing Rolando on the threshold through the peephole, was terrified. It turns out that Rolando had been watching him for some time, as the addict was determined to claim what he considered his or, otherwise, inform the authorities, pointing him out as a suspect in the previous disappearances.

Julio delicately placed the baby girl in her crib, his ragged breathing echoing in the room. A shiver ran down his spine as he made his way to the kitchen, each step resonating in the oppressive silence of the house. With trembling hands, he rummaged through the utensils until he found the knife he needed: short, sharp, perfect for his grim purpose.

He cautiously opened the front door, his heart pounding in his chest. Instead of greeting Rolando, who stood unsuspecting at the entrance, Julio acted with determination and precision. With a swift and accurate motion, he delivered a blow to Rolando's left intercostal space, a thrust worthy of the most skilled Italian fencers. Silence echoed through the house as the knife found its target: Rolando's heart.

Four agonizing seconds passed before Rolando collapsed to the floor, his life rapidly ebbing away. The dull sound of his body hitting the ground resonated in the kitchen, an ominous echo of the tragedy that had just occurred. Meanwhile, droplets of blood, like tears of the macabre act, splattered on the entrance floor where Rolando's lifeless body lay. Julio, with adrenaline coursing through his veins, didn't notice the bloodstain as the weight of his actions began to sink into his consciousness.

With a final sigh, Rolando joined his dismembered and beautiful wife. Together in eternal silence, they found the union that death had separated in life.

Subsequently, Julio moved the addict's corpse to the basement, placing it on the operating table to dismember and gradually extract pieces of the deceased, planning to distribute them in plastic bags and throw them into a nearby river. All the bags used in his criminal actions were black Glad brand, with a thirty-gallon capacity. He used the electric bone saw to section the spine at the neck level and placed the head with various limb segments in several bags. In total, five bags would complete the task of disposing of the deceased's body. Approximately three hours remained before Rosalinda returned from work. Julio hurried between cutting the pieces and caring for the kidnapped baby. He called Papote, who arrived and took away the Glad trash bags with Rolando's scattered remains. The third time was the charm for this unfortunate addict of life.

Upon returning home, Rosalinda noticed a small bloodstain on the entrance floor but didn't give it much importance, as another event held greater relevance: the new arrival. She immediately went to the room where the baby girl was resting, wrapped from head to toe in a pink kimono. She caressed and hugged her against her body. Julio greeted her with a kiss and informed her that they would be together at least two weeks until they found a foster home for the girl. When asked why not them, Julio avoided a direct response.

After leaving the baby asleep in the crib, "Julio, what is that bloodstain at the entrance?" Rosalinda asked. He quickly replied, "Oh, that... I pricked myself practicing surgical knots..." an explanation that intrigued Rosalinda.

No more than three days passed when a citizen spotted a pair of black bags floating in the waters of the Cialitos River. Two were found in the Cialitos, three in the Rio Balbas. Immediately notified to the authorities, they proceeded to inspect their contents. To their macabre surprise, they discovered human remains emanating a pungent odor of decomposition. The remains were transferred to the forensic institute for the corresponding investigation.

In a second bag, the victim's head was revealed. Using the dental impressions of the deceased, investigators identified Rodolfo, the addict who had survived an assassination attempt at the hospital while recovering from a drug overdose. Despite being under an unsupervised witness protection program, Rodolfo managed to leave his safe house three days earlier, thus meeting his tragic fate of dismemberment.

Forensic pathologists highlighted in the autopsy reports the precision of the cuts, comparable to amputations performed by certified surgeons in cases of gangrene. This detail suggests that the killer possesses extraordinary surgical skills.

With a police report detailing the recent disappearance of another child, agents Darío and Meléndez, along with attorney Carmen, plunged back into the investigation. They meticulously reviewed the information collected during the case of the baby's kidnapping in Ciales, including data provided by the coroner about the murder and dismemberment of Rodolfo.

They noted several details, such as the use of black Glad brand bags with the same weight used in previous cases involving the bodies of newborns. Additionally, they highlighted the serial killer's surgical skill. The connection between these cases and the presence of empty bodies in previous incidents suggested the possibility of an organ trade carried out by an organization with a strikingly similar plan. It was a mystery why there was a consonant surrounded by three dots inside the abdominal cavity of the cases as a distinctive signature. The perpetrator wanted to stand out with his art.

9

Upon waking up the next morning, Rosalinda immersed herself in a familiar routine as she bathed the baby girl, but she was palpably surprised when a flash of albino hair caught her attention. A delicately white strand peeked out among the baby's golden curls, evoking disturbing memories of her time in the maternity wing of the hospital. As the water gently fell over the baby's skin, Rosalinda couldn't take her eyes off that strand, so similar to the one belonging to the girl she had cared for with such love and dedication in the previous weeks.

Despite the charming nature of the little girl and her quick adaptation to her new home and foster parents, a feeling of unease began to grow in Rosalinda's heart. The connection between this baby and the one she had examined at the hospital became increasingly evident in her mind, awakening a series of unanswered questions and sowing the seed of mystery in her consciousness.

With a racing heartbeat, Rosalinda plunged into the dark fabric of the investigation, devouring every news story related to the disappearance of children with almost obsessive fervor. The echo of her own heartbeat filled the room as she felt overwhelmed by the avalanche of information, trying to connect the dots that resisted fitting together in her mind.

An internal struggle consumed her, like a whirlwind shaking her conscience and her loyalty towards her husband. What secrets was he keeping? And how much was she willing to discover to get to the truth? Every click of the mouse was one more step towards the abyss of uncertainty, as the darkness of her own doubts threatened to completely engulf her.

The shadow of suspicion loomed over her, transforming every corner of her home into a labyrinth of secrets and lies. Rosalinda found herself on a precipice, with fate hanging by a fragile thread, torn between loyalty to her husband and the growing awareness of the true nature of his actions.

To her surprise, she discovered the case from February of this year when she held little Panchito in her arms. Learning that

Agent Darío, in charge of the investigation, had not achieved significant results, she decided to contact him to obtain more information. Darío took the call with some suspicion, as it was uncommon for kidnappers to communicate with authorities to return their victims. Despite this unusual fact, he chose to interview Rosalinda, joined by Agent Meléndez and Carmen. Caution was essential to prevent Julio from discovering the investigation and opting for a more desperate action.

In the midst of the whirlwind of suspicions and speculations, a cloak of uncertainty covered everyone. Looks crossed loaded with doubts, conversations became ambiguous, and whispers multiplied like shadows in the twilight. In that labyrinth of mysteries and secrets, no one could say anything for sure.

Every step was a venture into darkness, every word a distorted echo in the void of distrust. Paranoia became the constant companion of each individual, weaving an invisible web that enveloped the entire community. Even the strongest bonds of friendship and trust wavered under the weight of uncertainty.

In that town shrouded in the shadow of suspicion, truth faded away among the cracks of confusion, leaving everyone in a state of bewilderment and fear. In a world where no one was sure of anything, danger lurked around every corner, waiting for its moment to reveal itself and change the course of the intertwined destinies of those who dwelled in the shadows of mystery.

With the weight of guilt crushing her and the fervent desire to end the dark chain of crimes plaguing her conscience, Rosalinda finally made a transcendent decision: to collaborate with the authorities as an informant. Every step forward on this perilous path was a battle against her own demons, but she was determined to face them bravely. Armed with the determination to redeem herself and bring justice for the innocent, she plunged into an ocean of risks and sacrifices.

Despite the fears that lurked around every corner, Rosalinda found an inner strength she didn't know she possessed. Every word shared with the authorities was a step towards light, a ray of hope in the darkness that had consumed her for too long.

Now, as an informant, she was ready to challenge fate and confront the monsters that had lurked in the shadows of her life. In her determination and courage, Rosalinda found a new reason to move forward, a reason to believe that even in the midst of chaos and despair, there was still hope for redemption and justice.

With the information provided by Rosalinda, detectives Darío and Meléndez meticulously outline the details of an undercover operation. Carmen, the lawyer, closely collaborates with the police to ensure that every aspect complies with legal regulations. The operation unfolds at a strategic point, though Julio is not present. As events unfold, Rosalinda faces the dilemma of her betrayal towards her husband. Doubt attacks her. There is always the possibility that it is all a hoax and not linked to the disappearances of other babies. However, the physical data that contributed to the identification of the dismembered babies, such as Panchito's mole and Isabel's fused fingers, are known to

Rosalinda, causing an abnormal increase in her heart rate.

Amidst the murky scenario of secrets and dangers, the fear of retaliation from Julio adds to Rosalinda's already overwhelming concerns. Although Julio does not display aggressive behavior in his daily life, the mere idea of confronting him, especially when he has a scalpel in his hands, is enough to send chills down her spine.

Every time Rosalinda found herself near Julio, a shadow of unease settled over her, reminding her of the potential danger he represented. The mask of apparent tranquility he wore concealed a dark and sinister enigma, fueling the fear of what he might be capable of if he felt threatened or betrayed.

However, Rosalinda knew she could not let fear paralyze her. With each passing day, her determination grew stronger, propelling her to move forward with her decision to collaborate with the authorities, no matter the risks involved. She knew that facing Julio would be a test of fire, but she was willing to risk it all for justice and truth.

The ticking of the clock ominously echoed in the air, marking the inexorable passage of time towards the date of the new organ delivery. For those desperate souls eagerly awaiting a second chance, the calendar had become an unforgiving reminder of their hopes and fears.

The needy had been meticulously informed about the moment they would receive the human portions that corresponded to them, a macabre process of synchronization destined to save lives at the expense of others. Some lay in hospital beds, submerged in a sleep induced by anesthesia, eagerly awaiting the crucial moment when a liver, a kidney, a heart, a lung, bone marrow, pancreas, or small intestine would be transplanted to restore their hope for a full life.

However, behind the facade of salvation and hope lurked a dark network of interests and secrets. Behind each organ offered in sacrifice lay a story of pain and tragedy, a trail of blood and suffering that stained red the seemingly benevolent process of organ donation.

For those trapped in this sinister game of life and death, the arrival of the organ delivery date represented not only an opportunity for survival but also the beginning of a new chapter in a story marked by desperation and desperate struggle for survival.

Aware of the fateful destiny awaiting the little guest under both their care, Rosalinda felt the overwhelming weight of responsibility on her shoulders. She knew that time was inexorably running out, like the clock of a bomb ticking away the seconds until its inevitable explosion.

The two-week deadline for the infant's stay in their home was rapidly approaching its end, and with it, the imminent threat of her delivery for Julio's dark purposes. Every day that passed was a step closer to the abyss, a step closer to the precipice from which the little one could not escape.

Rosalinda felt trapped in a race against time, fighting against time and her own fears to find a way to protect the innocent creature she cared for as if she were her own daughter. She knew she couldn't allow the girl to fall into Julio's hands, but the shadows of danger loomed menacingly over her, obstructing her path to salvation.

As the clock continued its relentless march, Rosalinda prepared to face her worst nightmare: the moment when she would have to say goodbye to the girl and leave her in the hands of the man whose sinister intentions threatened to consume them both. With her heart constricted by fear and anguish, she clung to the hope of finding a solution before it was too late.

In a clandestine meeting, detectives Darío and Meléndez, accompanied by lawyer Carmen, met with Rosalinda in a secluded location, away from prying eyes. The tension in the air was palpable as Rosalinda took a breath and provided a detailed layout of her home, outlining every corner with precision and meticulously describing Julio's schedules and routines.

--"You have to stop him before he harms the baby!"--, Rosalinda pleaded with a broken voice, her eyes filled with tears and palpable fear.

Fear was reflected in every gesture, in every word that escaped her lips, as she desperately clung to the hope of saving the girl from a fatal fate.

Darío solemnly nodded, his face hardened by determination.

--"We will do everything in our power, Rosalinda. But we need your help. Are you sure you're willing to confront him?"--.

Rosalinda nodded with determination, although her voice trembled slightly.

--"Yes, I am. I can't let this continue. Please promise me you'll protect the girl"--.

The detectives exchanged meaningful glances before Meléndez spoke up.

--"We promise you, Rosalinda. We'll do everything in our power to stop Julio and keep the girl safe. But we need to act quickly and precisely"--.

With a lump in her throat, Rosalinda nodded, knowing that time was running out and that every minute was crucial to the fate of the innocent child. Together, they prepared to face the danger lurking in the shadows, hoping that this time, justice would prevail over darkness.

The tension was palpable as everyone awaited the critical moment for Julio's capture. In the operating room of his basement, Julio moved with determination, preparing to carry out his nefarious procedure. Sharp instruments gleamed in the dim light, while the darkness of the place seemed to close around him like a sinister cloak.

Rosalinda, maintaining a facade of normality, watched every move Julio made with a mixture of fear and cunning. Every gesture, every word, was analyzed meticulously as she subtly signaled to the detectives about the proximity of the act. A fleeting glint in her eyes, a slight nod of her head, was enough to communicate the imminent arrival of the crucial moment.

The detectives, hidden nearby, received the signals attentively, preparing to act at the right moment. Adrenaline coursed through their veins as they remained alert, ready to burst onto the scene and put an end to Julio's dark plans.

In the midst of the tense wait, Rosalinda clung to the hope that, this time, justice would prevail over darkness. With her heart in her throat, she awaited the decisive moment, aware that the fate of the little girl was at stake and that she could not allow evil to triumph once more.

When darkness enveloped the house, a SWAT team, in perfect coordination with the detectives, stealthily moved toward the target. Every step was calculated, every movement executed with military precision, as the shadows enveloped them like a protective mantle.

Rosalinda, with an act of courage that defied the fear consuming her, managed to distract Julio. With carefully chosen words and calculated gestures, she kept his attention focused on her, diverting his gaze from the entrance to the basement where the agents moved stealthily.

Minutes turned into hours in the tense silence of the night as Rosalinda kept Julio occupied with her cunning. Every second was crucial, every breath held was an echo of the determination driving them forward.

Meanwhile, in the dark and claustrophobic basement, Julio held the baby in his arms, about to administer the nitrous oxide that would plunge her into a dangerous stupor. However, before he could complete his sinister plan, the door opened with a barely perceptible creak, revealing the macabre scene before them. The agents, with relentless precision, burst into the operating room, putting an end to Julio's dark plans before they could fully materialize. They caught him red-handed.

At the moment of the raid, Julio was taken aback by the sudden appearance of the agents in his surgical sanctuary. His face twisted in a mixture of surprise and desperation as he tried to react to the sudden threat to his macabre plan. Overwhelmed by panic, he attempted to resist with all his might but was quickly subdued by the overwhelming numerical and tactical superiority of the agents, who handcuffed him efficiently.

Rosalinda, watching with a lump in her throat as Julio was captured, experienced a mixture of relief and deep emotion. Despite having achieved the goal of stopping the dangerous criminal, she couldn't help but feel overwhelmed by the gravity of the situation and the consequences of Julio's dark acts. However, her primary focus was on ensuring the safety of the baby.

With trembling yet determined hands, Rosalinda approached the operating table where the little girl lay, verifying that she was unharmed and protecting her with love and determination. With every beat of her heart, she promised to protect her from any harm that might threaten her in the future, willing to sacrifice everything for her safety and well-being.

At the police station, Julio faced a tough interrogation. Surrounded by irrefutable evidence and confronted with Rosalinda's betrayal, the once defiant demeanor of the criminal crumbled under the relentless pressure of the evidence against him. With chilling coldness, he confessed to the entirety of his crimes, revealing the horrors of his acts without a trace of remorse.

The detectives watched with incredulity and repulsion as Julio recounted the macabre details of his actions, his words echoing in the interrogation room like the echo of pure evil. Each revelation was a direct blow to the hearts of those listening, exposing the twisted nature of the man who had been lurking in the shadows.

For Rosalinda, Julio's confession was a devastating blow, a brutal reminder of the darkness that had been so close to consuming her. Although she knew she had done the right thing by reporting him, the weight of the truth was overwhelming, leaving invisible scars on her soul.

As the criminal's words filled the room with their malevolent revelation, Rosalinda clung to the hope that, at last, justice would prevail over evil and that those who had been victims of Julio's crimes would find some kind of peace and comfort in knowing that the perpetrator had been brought to justice.

After Julio's capture, detectives Darío and Meléndez, along with Carmen, conducted a thorough search of Julio's basement operating room. Every dark corner and hiding place was carefully examined for evidence that could shed light on the sinister surgeon's dark crimes.

Among the findings, they discovered a computer hidden carefully behind a false wall. With expert hands, the detectives accessed it and came across a startling revelation: the "Ellipsis" program, a key tool in Julio's network of infant organ trafficking operating in the shadows.

Every line of code was a direct link to the horrors that had been perpetrated in that clandestine operating room. The coldness of the transactions recorded on the screen was a brutal reminder of the cruelty and greed driving Julio's macabre machinery.

For the detectives and lawyer Carmen, the discovery of the "Ellipsis" program was a crucial breakthrough in the investigation, a missing link that finally connected the dots in a network of corruption and evil. With renewed determination, they pledged to follow the trail of evidence to its ultimate consequences, ensuring that all responsible parties were brought to justice and that no victim was left voiceless.

In the darkness of the basement, the light of truth shone brighter than ever, illuminating the path to justice and the end of the nightmare that had consumed so many innocents.

While investigating the computer, a forensic computer technician managed to access the encrypted Ellipsis system.

"Look at this," he said in amazement, "this program records every organ request, with details of the recipients and delivery dates."

With this new evidence, the detectives confronted Julio during the interrogation.

"We know about Ellipsis, Julio. Everything is recorded here," said Darío, showing him the computer screen. Julio, feeling cornered by the reality of his situation, lowered his gaze, acknowledging the futility of continuing to deny his involvement.

Julio, finally broken, began to reveal how Ellipsis operated.

"Each request was encoded... A sequence of three dots... Confirmation, availability, and extraction..." he explained resignedly.

These confessions provided the detectives with a deeper understanding of the magnitude and sophistication of the operation.

Finally, Julio was brought to justice, where he faced a severe trial that exposed the horrifying extent of his crimes. With each testimony and every piece of evidence presented in the courtroom, the depth of his depravity and the devastation he had caused were revealed.

Rosalinda, despite having collaborated with the authorities to expose the horrors perpetrated by Julio, found herself engulfed in a whirlwind of conflicting emotions. Although she had made the brave decision to confront the darkness that had surrounded her life, she now faced the consequences of her own actions and decisions. The weight of guilt and doubt consumed her, leaving her trapped in a maze of remorse and anguish.

The little girl, unaware of the horrors that surrounded her, was returned to her biological parents, offering them a ray of hope after a period of unimaginable despair. For them, her return marked the beginning of a new life, full of love and care, far from the shadows of the past that had threatened to consume them.

Although time could not completely erase the emotional scars left by the traumatic experience, their daughter's presence reminded them that love, and hope are powerful forces capable of overcoming even the darkest moments.

For the little girl, returning home meant a return to the safety and warmth of a loving family environment. As she grew, surrounded by the love and care of her parents, the painful memories of her past began to fade, replaced by the joy and happiness of a future full of possibilities.

Although the road to healing would be long and difficult, the presence of the little girl in their lives was a constant reminder of the strength of the human spirit to overcome adversity and find light even in the darkest moments. In her innocent smile and joyful laughter, they found the promise of a better tomorrow, where love and hope would shine eternally.

With the information obtained from Ellipsis, the detectives were able to identify several members of the network, including Papote, and planned his capture. The evidence also allowed them to trace the fate of the organs and connect the cases of missing babies with Julio's network.

Armed with this critical information, the detectives and the police mobilized to capture Papote, Julio's cunning accomplice. Although he had managed to stay in the shadows for a long time, the network he had woven with Julio was quickly crumbling.

In an urgent meeting at the police station, detectives Darío and Meléndez, along with Carmen, discussed their next move.

"Papote is elusive, but without Julio, it's only a matter of time before he makes a mistake," argued Meléndez.

"He must be captured before he tries to flee or worse, continues with his activities," added Darío.

Rosalinda, still recovering from the shock of the recent events, was summoned by the detectives.

"Rosalinda, any information about Papote could be crucial," insisted Carmen.

"I know it's difficult for you, but we need your help to catch him."

Rosalinda, with a trembling voice, responded:

"I know he used to meet at an abandoned warehouse at pier two, near a short landing strip. Julio mentioned something about it once."

With the critical information obtained from Ellipsis, law enforcement was able to locate Papote in an abandoned warehouse, a place that had served as a central point in his illicit operations. It had the advantage of a short landing strip nearby. A team of specialized agents, including the experienced detective

Darío, meticulously prepared for the operation. Armed and with a clear strategy, they surrounded the building, closing off all possible escape routes.

Papote, who had always lived one step ahead of the law, quickly realized he was cornered. In a desperate attempt to evade capture, he opted for the most dangerous route: confrontation. Armed and dangerous, he headed towards a little-known back exit, skillfully dodging the shadows and dark corners of the warehouse.

At the critical moment, as the agents closed in to secure the perimeter, Papote emerged with surprising speed. He drew his weapon with cold and calculating skill, firing controlled bursts that wounded two of the agents in the sudden chaos. Tension soared to the maximum; shouts and orders echoed in the tense air of the confrontation.

Darío, with years of experience in high-risk situations, remained calm despite the imminent danger. At a crucial moment, as Papote turned to aim directly at him, Darío, with lethal precision, fired his 9-millimeter Glock pistol. The bullet found its mark in

Papote's temporal region. Time seemed to stand still as Papote collapsed to the ground, his life slipping away in an instant. It was the first time Darío had killed a person.

The place fell into a sepulchral silence, broken only by the agents' ragged breaths and the distant wail of reinforcement sirens. Papote's fall marked the end of an era of terror and crime, but at a cost that would weigh on the minds and hearts of all involved.

10

As Rosalinda faced her own demons and began her path to redemption, an act of hope and love unfolded in parallel. Little Isabelita, the innocent caught in the midst of a dark scheme, was about to be returned to the loving arms of her true parents, Víctor, and Rosa.

Rosalinda, accompanied by Detectives Darío and Meléndez along with Carmen, headed to the home of Víctor and Rosa, a place marked by the absence of their beloved daughter. Upon arrival, the air was charged with a mixture of anxiety and hope.

"We've come to bring you Isabelita," announced Rosalinda with a soft but firm voice, carefully holding the little girl in her arms.

The moment Rosalinda handed Isabelita to her parents was filled with pure emotion. Rosa, with tears of joy and relief streaming down her cheeks, took her daughter into her arms, embracing her with overflowing love. Víctor, with a smile lighting up his face marked by recent pain, joined the embrace, forming a perfect circle of reunited family.

"I'm so sorry for what you've had to go through," murmured Rosalinda, her eyes also brimming with tears.

"Isabelita has been safe, and I made sure she received all the love and care she deserves."

Víctor, looking at Rosalinda, responded with gratitude: "Thank you for taking care of her. Despite everything, it's a comfort to know she was in good hands."

As Rosalinda walked away from Víctor and Rosa's house, she felt a weight lift from her heart. Isabelita restoration to her parents was a small but significant step in her quest for redemption. Although the road ahead was filled with uncertainty, she knew that every act of kindness and justice was a step towards healing, both for herself and for those affected by Julio's actions.

With the closure of this dark chapter, the community could begin to heal. Rosalinda, though legally exonerated, faced her own internal battle, grappling with guilt and the knowledge of her unwitting complicity. The story concludes with a reflection on the lasting impact of these events, both on the victims and on those who, in one way or another, found themselves entangled in this web of horror and despair.

As the sun set, painting the sky with warm and melancholic hues, Rosalinda sat alone in her garden, now overly quiet and empty. The shadows of the evening danced gently on the lawn, reflecting the turbulence of her thoughts.

The fresh evening air caressed her face, bringing with it a rush of emotions and memories. The betrayal of her husband Julio, whom she had once loved and trusted blindly, echoed in her mind like a persistent echo. Her complicity, though unintended, in the horrors perpetrated by Julio, pursued her relentlessly.

--"How could I have been so blind?"--, she asked herself again and again, her voice barely a whisper among the trees.

In her chest, a broken heartbeat with the weight of guilt and remorse. The image of

Julio, now a distant memory behind bars, intertwined with the innocent faces of the children affected by his crimes.

--"Never again"--, she promised herself, a pledge that would become her beacon on the path to redemption. It would take a long time before she could forgive Julio, who was consumed in prison.

With a newfound determination, Rosalinda decided to dedicate her life to helping victims of similar crimes. She would become a voice for those who had been silenced, a tireless advocate for the innocent and vulnerable. She felt a burning urgency to do something meaningful, to turn her pain and experience into a force for good.

In the days and weeks that followed, Rosalinda began working with local organizations supporting victims of abduction and trafficking. She shared her story, not seeking sympathy, but offering empathy and understanding. In every face she encountered, she saw an opportunity to make a difference, to somehow make up for the mistakes of the past.

As night settled in, a sense of peace and purpose began to bloom in Rosalinda's soul. Though the path to redemption was fraught with challenges, she was determined to walk it with courage. This new stage of her life didn't erase her past, but it offered a fresh start, an opportunity to sow hope in the midst of desolation.

As the stars began to shine in the night sky, Rosalinda sighed deeply, allowing herself to believe in the possibility of a future where love and compassion could heal even the deepest wounds.

The ellipsis became the sinister mark that both mutilated bodies and the computer program used in organ trafficking, leaving an ominous imprint of horror and depravity in the dark corners of criminality.

***

About the Author

Born on April 14, 1954, in San Juan, Puerto Rico, Dr. Humberto Lugo Vicente, better known as Tito Lugo, is a distinguished figure in the field of pediatric surgery. His career has been marked by a fervent commitment to both medicine and the community he serves.

During his education at Colegio San José de Río Piedras, Dr. Lugo Vicente not only excelled in his studies but also led the local rock band "The Red Stones". He demonstrated exceptional skills in areas as varied as music and martial arts, achieving black belts in Shotokan and brown belts in Taekwondo. His efforts to finance his education in karate, through selling newspapers and other jobs, reflect his early commitment to his goals.

Graduating Magna Cum Laude from the University of Puerto Rico in Sciences, specializing in Chemistry and Biochemistry, Dr. Lugo Vicente was recognized with the Chemistry Medal and the Facundo Bueso Medal for his outstanding academic performance. He continued to shine in his medical studies at the same university, graduating as a member of Alpha Omega Alpha, the medical honor society.

Dr. Lugo Vicente has made a mark in pediatric surgery throughout his career. He completed his specialization in General and Pediatric Surgery at the University of Puerto Rico. He then joined the faculty as a Professor of Pediatric Surgery. His commitment to excellence in education led him to occupy various leadership positions, including President of the Medical Faculty and Director of the Surgery Department at the University Pediatric Hospital.

Dr. Lugo Vicente has been a tireless advocate for the improvement of medical services in Puerto Rico, particularly in his fight to equip the University Pediatric Hospital with modern operating rooms. This has benefited countless children and families.

Outside of his medical career, he enjoys a fulfilling family life with his wife Wanda Torres Otero and their four children: Karlos, Alex, Javier, and María del Carmen. His dedication to community welfare and passion for medicine continue to be a source of inspiration for new generations.

Currently, Dr. Lugo Vicente practices at his private office in San Jorge Hospital and the University Pediatric Hospital. There, he provides quality medical care while cultivating his interests in sports, writing, and enology, always maintaining the balance and moderation that characterize his life philosophy.

Other novels from the Author
https://www.amazon.com/author/titolugo.md

1- Aquamistic (Spanish and English)
2- El Gran Sueño / The Great Dream
3- Marca de Faraón / Mark of Pharaoh
4- La Isla del Retiro / The Island of Retirement
5- Espejismos en la Red / Digital Deceptions
6- Voces del Silencio / Voices of Silence
7- Travos... (Spanish and English)
8- Misericordia Letal / Lethal Mercy
9- "Pirulo..."(Spanish and English)
10- ...Elipsis... / ...Ellipsis...